Heaven's Kitchen

Monica Marks

Published by Trellis Publishing, 2021.

This is a work of fiction. Similarities to real people, places, or events are entirely coincidental.

HEAVEN'S KITCHEN

First edition. July 16, 2021.

ISBN: 979-8224280322

Written by Monica Marks.

HEAVEN'S KITCHEN

MONICA MARKS

<u>Heaven's Kitchen</u>

The dish sat, unmoving for a full minute and out of the corner of her eye, she caught Ryan's smirk.

Here it comes, she thought, opening her mouth before the head chef could.

"Kate, table three's order has been up for two minutes!" Beth barked, her eyes narrowing through the serving window. "Get to it, please!"

The waitress hurried forward, shooting the sous chef an apologetic smile as she scooped the plate off the stainless-steel countertop and rushed away without a word.

I'll apologize for speaking so harshly to her when we're alone, Beth promised herself but she knew Kate didn't take it personally. It was one of the prerequisites of working in a restaurant, after all. One needed to have thick skin.

One of these days, I'll have to grow some too, Beth thought wryly.

"You need to yell louder if you want them to move faster," Ryan told her, smirking slightly. Beth ignored him, knowing that he was about to make some jab about her ancestry as he always did.

"It works for you guys in the kitchen, doesn't it?" Ryan added.

"She got to the order just fine," Beth reminded him, turning back to the onions she was sautéing on the grill. She didn't want to fight about timing or anything else but Ryan hadn't finished his lecture yet.

"She should have gotten it the minute you put it down," the head chef insisted. "Now watch, the customer is going to send it back because it's cold and they you'll have to do it all over again."

"Or she can throw it in the microwave!" one of the other sous chef's quipped, only to receive a scathing look from Ryan. Beth stifled a sigh and shrugged. She knew that Ryan was only trying to make her a better chef but his methods didn't always jive with her disposition. Sometimes she wondered if working in the kitchen was a bad fit for her, particularly when the voices got loud and nerves got frayed.

"Come on, Bethy," Ryan continued, leering at her through his peripheral vision as he, too, worked on an order. "You've been out in the world now for eight years. It's time you left those Amish roots behind once and for all. I'd pay good money to hear you drop a four-letter word, just once."

"ME TOO!" came the collective chorus around her. Beth snorted and shook her head, feeling her shoulders drop slightly. The lecture portion was over. They were on to the joking part of the afternoon.

"That's not going to happen," she replied, laughing. Ryan was teasing her but sometimes, she felt like she might not ever fit in with the Englisch. It wasn't anything specific that he said or did. No one overtly went out of their way to make her feel ill at ease but it was built into her and no matter what Beth did, she couldn't seem to shake the feeling.

You're an Englischer now, she reminded herself for what was probably the thousandth time. She wondered, then, why she never quite felt right among them. It was one of the reasons she had opted to stay in New York City, after all. The place was a melting pot of cultures, people flocking there from all walks of life. It seemed a good a place as any to start a new life without seeming like an outcast.

You love your life here, she growled silently and that was also true. The city offered her so much more than the district in upstate New York ever could have. The adventure she'd sought, the experience of working as an independent woman, not the wife of some Amish farmer.

Guilt shot through her at the thought.

Your sister is the wife of an Amish farmer, she remembered. *And so are many of your friends.*

But Beth was neither her sister nor any of the people she had left behind in Chautauqua. Somehow, the notion of remaining in the district, adhering to the ways of the Ordnung had been insurmountable to her and when she had left for Rumspringa when she turned sixteen, she had never returned.

"What are you shaking your head at?" Ryan demanded. "You don't believe me? I'm going to turn you into a proper chef yet, cursing and all. You'll make Gordon Ramsey blush by the time I'm done with you."

Beth giggled and threw her dark head of hair back to meet his eyes with mischievous green irises.

"You haven't succeeded in almost a decade," she joked and Ryan feigned a look of hurt.

"That's because you won't see me outside of work," he replied slyly. "If I got to take you on a date..."

"The answer is still no," she replied flatly and the kitchen staff erupted in snickers around them as Ryan scowled.

"Shot down again, Ry," Kevin sniggered. "When are you ever going to learn?"

"Probably never," Ryan sighed, winking at Beth and she grinned back at him. The endless and sometimes raunchy banter of the commercial kitchen was almost commonplace now. She knew that the men and women in her midst were her friends, even if they often said or did questionable things.

The fact was Beth Troyer wasn't in Chautauqua anymore. She was a chef in New York City, right where she was supposed to be.

~ ~ ~

"Beth, dear, you have a letter," Mrs. Connolly called out when she entered the house. Dropping her knapsack by the door, Beth hurried into the kitchen where her landlady sat, sipping on a cup of tea.

"Would you like a cup, dear?" she asked kindly and Beth gave the woman a warm smile.

"Yes, please," she replied. "But I can get it myself."

"You've been working all day, dear," Mrs. Connolly said, nodding toward the envelope on the table. "Sit down and I'll fix you a cup."

Gratefully, Beth did as she was instructed, reaching for the letter written in her mother's elegant script. A pang of remorse touched her gut as she realized she hadn't written to Anna in weeks, despite her promise to keep in touch. Her life had simply gotten too busy.

You should always have time for your family, a small voice in the back of her head nagged her. Beth instantly silenced it and tore open the envelope, pulling out the pages inside. Instantly, the half-smile that had rested on her face faltered entirely.

"Oh..." she murmured as Mrs. Connolly placed a steaming mug in front of her.

"Is everything all right, dear?"

Beth wasn't sure how to answer the question, her eyes scanning the disturbing words in front of her.

Dear Beth,

We haven't spoken in a long while. I know you must be very busy with your life and I don't want to interrupt but I thought you should know that your vedder has decided to sell the bakery. He will be announcing his retirement on the 25th of September. I realize you are occupied with work but it would mean a great deal to him if you could be there. As you know, the bakery has been in our familye for over a hundred years. Saying goodbye to the store will be difficult and he will need all the support he can garner.

If you are able to attend and this letter finds you in time, there is no need to inform us that you will be coming. As you know, there is always a place for you at our table and at the house. If you cannot make it, we will understand as we always have.

With Affection,

Mamm

Confusion and worry overcame Beth as she allowed the letter to fall to the table, her eyes narrowing.

"Beth?" She realized that Mrs. Connolly was staring at her, waiting for a response to her earlier inquiry. "Are you all right?"

She managed a brief smile, nodding at the elderly landlady from whom Beth had rented a room for five years.

"I just learned that my father is selling his bakery back home," she said slowly. "It has been in our family for a century."

"Oh my," Mrs. Connolly said, surprise coloring her face. "I wonder why he would do that."

"So do I," Beth agreed, rising slowly.

"Where are you going, dear? You haven't touched your tea!"

"I need to arrange some time off from work," she told Mrs. Connelly. "It looks like I'm going home for the weekend."

~ ~ ~

It was an eight-hour bus ride from New York's Grand Central Station to Chautauqua. Beth was on the only bus leaving the following day, a simple bag packed for an extended weekend as she bid adieu to her landlady and friends at the restaurant. Ryan had not given her a modicum of complaint when she'd asked for the time off, despite the short notice.

"You haven't called in sick once since you started working here," the head chef declared. "If I could bottle your work ethic and sell it, I would be a billionaire. Of course you can take the time to be with your family. Just don't come home with all those good habits I've tried so hard to squeeze out of you."

Beth had laughed and agreed but as she found herself alone with her thoughts on the long Greyhound ride, her anxiety began to mount. It made little sense to her that Caleb Troyer would even consider selling the shop that had been their family's pride. True, she hadn't been home in several years but she couldn't envision a circumstance which would cause him to think in selling terms.

Is he taking leave of his senses?

If that were the case, her mother would surely step in and make him realize what a mistake it would be yet her letter seemed complacent, accepting of what was to come.

By the time the bus pulled into the tiny depot in Chautauqua, Beth was a bundle of questioning nerves.

She stepped off the vehicle, reaching for her small case that the driver had unloaded on the curb. No sooner had she grabbed for it did she hear someone call out her name.

"Beth Troyer!"

She spun around, her short dark hair fanning around her face as her eyes rested on the bewildered Amish girl hurrying toward her.

"It *is* you!" Rachel cried, throwing her arms around her childhood friend. Beth laughed awkwardly and returned Rachel's embrace before setting her back to look at her. "I can't believe it! *Wat* are you doing here?"

"Visiting my *familye*," Beth replied quickly, her own Pennsylvania Dutch brogue quickly surfacing the presence of someone speaking her native tongue.

How long has it been since I've spoken Deitsch? And still, it rolls off the tongue.

Beth wasn't sure if that was a good thing or bad.

"*Mein Gotte*, Beth. Look at you! A true Englischer now, aren't you?" Rachel went on, smiling admiringly at her but Beth felt an unexpected defensiveness at the words, even though she was sure her friend meant no malice.

"You'll have to come for *nachtesse* and regale us with tales of living in the city. I still can't believe you were the only one of us who didn't come back to get baptized."

"I wish I could come for supper but I'm only here for a couple of days," Beth told her regretfully. She paused, unsure of how much of the town knew about her father's impending sale. Her mother had said he intended to announce it on Saturday. That was still two days away and she didn't want to disclose more than she was supposed to know.

"Aw, too bad. Eli will be disappointed he missed you," Rachel said.

Beth's brow raised, a slight shiver running through her at the mention of the familiar name.

"Eli Wagner?"

"*Ja*," Rachel tittered. "We got married two years ago. We have a *boppli*, Leah."

"Oh, Rachel, that's wonderful!" Beth sighed. A strange feeling struck her gut, causing her stomach to shift uncomfortably.

Is that jealously I'm feeling? Ridiculous!

She was happy for her friend and for Eli who had always loved Rachel, even when they were children.

The same way someone used to love you.

She quieted the reminder. Those days were long passed. Thinking about them would only open old wounds that had never really healed properly.

"Are you sure you can't come? At least for *kaffi*? I just made fresh *obrigoshe eepies*."

Beth's mouth inadvertently began to water at the mention of Rachel's famous cookies.

"Are you still selling those at my father's bakery?" she asked and Rachel giggled again.

"*Ja*. He keeps me busy. Especially now..."

Her smile fell slightly, trailing off as if she'd said too much and Beth realized she had an opening to ask questions.

"How is he doing?" Beth wanted to know. "Is he...happy?"

The question seemed lame after it left her lips but Beth wasn't sure what it was she needed to know about the circumstances surrounding the sale.

Rachel's mouth parted slightly and she sighed.

"I'm sure you know all about it," she muttered. "But I still feel disloyal discussing it."

Beth waited, a prickle of sweat form under her hairline.

"He's doing as well as can be expected," Rachel went on. "But it's all too much for him."

Too much? Why? Because he's getting older?

That didn't make sense. Aaron Troyer was far from an old man, he and his wife having their children when they were in their earlies twenties themselves. Beth was the youngest at twenty-four.

"Of course we have all tried our best to help but Anna is at her wits' end now," Rachel continued to explain. Beth bit on her lower lip. Whatever was happening was worse than she thought but she dared not press Rachel for details. It was humiliating to know she had been kept in the dark so long.

"I need to get home to Leah," Rachel said suddenly, perhaps sensing the change in her friend's face. "But say you will come for a short visit. Oh, and Amos is staying with us too."

An unexpected shiver of excitement flowed through Beth's body as she stared at Rachel, her mind turning.

"Oh?" she asked innocently. "Has he not married?"

Rachel chuckled.

"Eli keeps hoping he will if only to get him out of the house. My *mann* wants to have another *boppli* but with Amos about, there is no room."

Amos isn't married.

Beth reminded herself that it didn't matter. Her life wasn't in the district anymore. As soon as she got to the bottom of what was happening with her family, she was returning to New York, to her real life.

But it wouldn't hurt to say hello to your former beau, would it?

"Beth?"

She brought herself back to the present, the memories of a childhood romance whispering on the edges of her mind.

"*Ja*," Beth said quickly. "I'll come for a visit. Tomorrow? After noon?"

"Perfect! I will tell Eli!"

As Rachel hurried away, Beth found herself hoping that her friend would tell Amos too.

~ ~ ~

The relief on Anna Troyer's face was almost palpable when her eyes rested on her younger daughter.

"You came!" she breathed, tears of happiness filling her gaze. Shame seized Beth in a torrent.

"*Ja*, of course," she said quickly, stepping forward across the threshold. "How are you, *Mamm*?"

Anna shook her head, seeming unable to find her voice and worry overwhelmed Beth.

"*Mamm*, what is going on?" she demanded, setting her suitcase down in the entranceway, closing the door before anymore fall leaves could slip inside. "Why is Daed selling the bakery?"

Anna exhaled a breath that Beth was sure she'd been holding for months.

"Kumme. I'll make kaffi and we'll talk," she urged. Beth obeyed, following her mother into the back of the house. There was something different about the modest two-storey building in which she had been raised but as Beth looked about, she couldn't quite figure out what it was.

The furniture seemed the same and while there were different throws and carpets about the house, they didn't account for the feeling that was creeping up on Beth.

It has nothing to do with the décor. There's a sensation in here I don't understand.

Anna gestured for her to sit and Beth sank to the table, watching as her mother lit the stove and placed a cast iron kettle on top. She purposely avoided Beth's eyes.

"Have you seen your *schwedere* yet?" Anna asked. Beth could tell she was avoiding the question her daughter had posed.

"Nee," Beth replied. "I came straight here from the bus station."

"If had known you were coming, I would have had Miriam come for you."

Beth's brow furrowed.

"Is Daed at the bakery?" she asked. Anna stopped fussing at the counter and splayed her hands against the wood, taking a deep breath before she raised her head.

"Nee, Bethy. He's upstairs."

"Upstairs?" she echoed, rising from her place but her mother motioned for her to sit down.

"He's resting, Beth. Don't disturb him."

Apprehension shot down her spine but Beth didn't sit.

"Why is he resting in the middle of a workday, *Mamm*?" she breathed but even as she asked the question, she knew the answer.

On the stove, the water began to boil and Anna turned to tend to it. Beth spun and hurried up the stairs, determined to see her father.

"BETH!" Anna yelled but the younger woman ignored her and knocked on the closed door of her parents' bedroom. There was no answer and as Anna's footfalls neared, Beth threw the door open.

"Oh *mein Gotte*..." Beth whimpered, tears filling her eyes as she took in the scene before her. As her mother had warned, her father was, indeed, asleep on the bed, wrapped in two thick quilts but even so, she could see how much weight he'd lost since she'd last seen him. On the bedside were several prescription bottles and the heavy scent in the room told Beth that Aaron had been bedridden for a long while.

A warm hand fell on her shoulder and Anna pulled her daughter back, closing the door behind her.

"I told you, he's resting," Anna murmured. Beth spun and gaped accusingly at her mother.

"What is wrong with him?" she cried. "Why didn't you tell me he was so sick?"

"Shh!" Anna growled, pressing her finger to her lips and gesturing for Beth to follow her back downstairs. "He barely gets enough rest as it is. I won't have you waking him now."

Begrudgingly, Beth returned to the main floor where she began to pace the kitchen.

"Why is he so sick? Why didn't you tell me?" she demanded again. Anna gave her a stoic look.

"You haven't been in touch, Bethy," she said simply. Beth's temper flared.

"That's your excuse? You didn't tell me that Daed is sick because I haven't written?"

"*Nee, lieb*. He didn't want me to tell you anything. If he had his way, Miriam wouldn't know either but given the size of this district..."

"Miriam should have told me!"

Beth was indignant, furious at everyone, including herself.

If I had come home more often, I would have known.

"This is why he's selling the bakery."

It wasn't a question but finally an understanding of what was going on.

"He has Stage Four liver cancer, *liebling*. He is determined to die at home, as he should."

"D-die?!" Beth sputtered.

"He is trying to get his affairs in order before he meets Gotte," Anna went on, pouring a cup of tea for her daughter. There was a resignation to her voice, one that told Beth that she had come to terms with what was happening long ago.

I should have been here. I should be here.

"I can't handle the bakery alone," Anna said. "Gotte knows, I don't have yours or your father's culinary skills. Neither does Miriam although she has tried her best. If not for Rachel Byler, we would have been out of business long ago. Selling is the right thing to do. It will give me enough money to invest in a new business."

She has really thought about this.

Anna slid the cup in front of her daughter, cupping her cheek casually as she sat back.

"I'm sorry you're learning about this now, Bethy but it is the way your vedder wanted it. You have your own life and he respected that."

Miserably, Beth sank back into her chair, tears welling in her eyes as she willed herself not to cry.

This used to be my life once too, she thought, the pain of all she'd learned overcoming her. *But I let that all go for what?*

But even as the warmth of the tea filled her stomach, Beth was sure she'd never feel comfort again.

~ ~ ~

The following morning, Beth was shocked to learn her father had gone into town.

"I-should he be doing that?"

"He has appointments to keep," Anna told her nonchalantly. "And arguing with him is like arguing with a *geess*. He's certainly as stubborn as a goat. Go see Miriam and I'm sure your *vedder* will be home by the time you return."

Beth considered staying close to the house but the more time she spent there, the more suffocated she felt.

On the other hand, she wasn't sure she wanted to see her sister either. She knew visiting with Miriam would only lead to an endless judgmental lecture on how she'd disappointed everyone.

Rachel. I'll go to Rachel.

The last hints of summer lingered in the morning air and normally, the weather would have made Beth smile but that day, her heart was far too heavy to enjoy the sunshine. She walked the familiar roads toward Rachel's house but when she arrived, she was surprised to find no one home.

Didn't Mamm say Rachel has been helping at the bakery? Maybe that's where she is.

"*Hallo?*"

She spun at the unexpected voice, her eyes widening when she caught sight of a strappingly handsome young man, his red hair flowing to his shoulders, resting just over his suspenders. Her heart leapt into her throat.

"Amos," she breathed. For a moment, he only stared at her and Beth was sure he was going to storm away but to her utter relief, he strode closer, a wry smile toying on his lips.

"Rachel said you were back in town," he offered. "How are you, Beth?"

She opened her mouth to give a customary response but before she could, a strangled sob escaped her lips. To her horror, tears began to zigzag down her face before she even registered the fact that she was crying. Amos gaped at her, seeming as shocked as she was by the display but instead of scowling, he moved forward to embrace her.

"*Ja,*" he sighed. "I know about your *vedder.*"

His words only caused her to cry harder and Amos squeezed her gently toward him. The comfort of his warm arms brought her back to a time when life had been so much simpler.

Why had I ever wanted to escape that? She wondered irrelevantly.

"H-how long has he been sick?" Beth asked when she could finally find her voice. She dropped her head back to look at her childhood friend, her boyfriend from what felt like a million years ago now.

And yet, he feels so familiar, so right like no time has elapsed at all.

Amos had matured wonderfully and Beth, despite all her anguish, wondered if he thought the same about her. His bright blue eyes seemed to indicate that he did, his irises tracing the lines of her face like he was trying to memorize them.

"I'm not sure how long it's been since he was diagnosed," Amos told her. "He hid it for a long while but everyone could see he wasn't well for at least six months."

"They never told me," Beth muttered.

"Understandably," Amos agreed. She scowled.

"Just because I am living away from the district, doesn't mean I don't care about my family," she snapped, wriggling out of his arms. He shrugged.

"You made a new life for yourself, Beth and left the rest of us behind. You can't fault your father for thinking that you had forgotten about him."

Hurt and despair flowed through Beth's veins.

He's not just talking about Daed. He's talking about himself too. He thinks I abandoned everyone. And I did, didn't I?

How had it happened? She had never been selfish or self-absorbed. Beth had always loved her family, even if she had never seen herself settling in the community.

And yet, Amos was speaking the truth. She hadn't made an effort for any of them.

"You're still angry with me," she mumbled, dropping her head in shame.

"*Nee*, Beth. I was never really angry with you. Yes, I missed you terribly when you didn't return but I'm happy you found your way. That's what Rumspringa is for."

She bit on her lower lip and shook her head.

"What?" Amos asked.

"*Nee*," she muttered. "I don't think I found my way at all. I think I lost it."

Amos extend his arms and Beth sank her head back against his chest, relishing the strong, even sound of his heartbeat.

"It's not too late to find your way again," he whispered but in that moment, she had no idea how to do that.

~ ~ ~

"*Mein Gotte*, Bethy!" Rachel sighed, hurrying up the porch with a small child in her arms. "If I'd known you would be here so early, I would have come back much sooner!"

"I kept her entertained," Amos chuckled from his rocking chair and Beth gave him a wan smile.

"I just needed to get out of the house," she explained. "It's very dark in there."

"*Ja*," Rachel said sympathetically. Beth could see how tired her friend was and she immediately jumped up from her spot to take little Leah from her arms.

"*Hallo, lieb*," she murmured, smiling at the toddler. Leah laughed and threw her arms affectionately around Beth's neck as if she could sense the woman's need for comfort.

"Oh, *danke*," Rachel said gratefully, opening the door with her free arms. "Eli will be home soon and then I will need to get back to the bakery. One of the girls didn't show up today so Amelia Schroeder is watching the store but she doesn't know how to do anything. I only have a few minutes—"

"I'll go to the bakery," Beth interjected.

"*Ja*. You can come too," Rachel agreed from the threshold.

"*Nee*, I mean, I'll go run the bakery tonight. You stay home with your *familye*."

Amos and Rachel both gaped at her.

"You?" Rachel echoed and Beth laughed.

"I was more or less raised inside that *kucke*," she reminded them. "And I am a sous chef in New York. I can handle it."

"*Ja*," Rachel said slowly, her eyes darting toward her brother-in-law. "*Ja*, you can, can't you?"

Beth pretended not to understand what the look was about but she knew exactly what her friend was thinking.

Beth wondered if she wasn't thinking the same thing herself.

~ ~ ~

Rachel, Eli, Leah, and Amos came into the bakery at closing time. On their heels was Beth's father, looking as emaciated and sickly as she'd ever seen him.

"*Daed*!" she cried, running to embrace him.

"*Lieb*. I am so happy you're here."

Beth nodded, blinking away the fresh onset of tears filling her eyes. She didn't want to cry in front of him.

"How did it go this afternoon?" Rachel asked, setting Leah onto the floor as Beth studied her father closely.

"I had forgotten how calm a restaurant could be," Beth chuckled. "This certainly is a change of pace from New York."

She found herself blushing as her eyes met with Amos who was studying her with interest.

Very different than New York. In more ways than one. In better ways than one.

The thought was shocking. It seemed impossible that she would miss the tiny town in which she'd grown up but in the day that she'd been home, she'd been surrounded by constant reminders of what she'd been missing.

How did I not see it? Was I blinded by the chaos and lights of New York?

But everything was there in Chautauqua. Her family, her friends, the bakery that belonged in her family, not sold to some nameless, faceless corporation that would likely strip it and turn it into some character-lacking hole in the wall.

Rachel gasped from behind the counter where she was reading the cash printout for the day.

"This was calm?" she demanded, pulling her eyes to look at the bare racks around them. "I think this is better than my best day in sales."

Aaron laughed gently.

"That's my Beth," he said affectionately, his eyes warm and approving. "She could sell ice to a polar bear."

Beth shrugged.

"There is a demand for this bakery in town," she replied, ambling back toward her father. "You can't sell it."

Aaron's smile faded and he looked away but Beth didn't miss the slightly annoyed expression on his face.

"Beth, your *midder* told me that she had discussed my condition with you," he growled in a low voice. "Decision needed to be made—"

"You made those decisions before informing me," Beth interjected. "You made these choices based on the resources available to you."

Aaron lifted his head and eyed her blankly.

"What are you saying?"

Beth took a deep breath, waiting for the warning that would stop her from saying the next words but it didn't come.

I want to do this. I want to come home.

"I can run the bakery," she told him. There was a collective gasp but to her surprise, Aaron shook his head.

"That is only a temporary solution," he muttered. "What about when you return to New York?"

A slow, cautious smile formed on her lips.

"What if I don't return to New York, *Daed*?"

"You're going to stay?!" Rachel exclaimed and clapped her hands together with excitement. Aaron didn't look convinced.

"*Lieb*," he said in a low voice. "You aren't speaking with your right mind right now. You're talking out of pity. When the time comes for me to meet *Gotte*, you will be resentful of the fact that you stayed here and you will want to return to New York."

Beth shook her head, her peripheral vision taking in Amos who seemed to be hanging off her every word.

"*Nee, Daed*," she told him softly. "I don't think that's true."

She deliberately raised her head and met Amos' eyes.

"I think all this time, I have been going through the motions of living but I lost sight of the most important thing—love. I haven't felt the warmth of my *familye* or *freind* in years and somehow, I never noticed. That is not how I was raised and it is never what I wanted for myself. Yet, I live a quiet, solitary life."

She paused, swallowing the lump forming in her throat.

"Please, *Daed*, let me stay and run the bakery. I will speak to Bishop Albrecht about being baptized if the district will still have me."

"Really, Bethy?" Rachel squealed again. Leah, not understanding anything but her mother's excitement, also squeaked in delight. Beth had to laugh through the film of tears in her eyes.

"*Ja*, really," she insisted, watching as her father's dubiousness melted away. Relief overcame her and she exhaled, knowing that he was about to accept her proposal.

"What about your life in New York?" Amos called out, his voice jarring Beth slightly. She had almost forgotten that he was still there. She gave him a tentative smile.

"Weren't you listening? I have no life in New York. My life is here."

She eyed him meaningfully but she could see that Amos would not be so easily convinced.

I don't fault him for doubting me. I left him once but I won't do it again.

"Aaron, say you'll accept her terms!" Rachel cried out when a heavy silence hung between them. "She is waiting for your answer!"

Beth's father dropped his head solemnly.

"You have no idea how long I have hoped to hear you say those words," he choked. "*Ja*, of course you can run the bakery. It is your legacy, after all."

Again, father and daughter embraced and Beth allowed the tears to freely fall down her face.

It was time to start again. This time, she would not forget how blessed she was.

~ ~ ~

The clang of pots almost overrode Rachel's voice calling out to her but Beth caught the sound of her voice on her friend's lips.

"Bethy! There's a man here looking for you!"

Beth set the baking pan down on the counter and nodded to another chef.

"Finish that please," she told her before wiping her hands on her apron and making her way into the dining room. Her movements were slightly awkward as she pushed through the new doors separating the kitchen from the front.

Almost instantly, her eyes rested on the visitor, sticking out like a sore thumb in his hipster attire. He whooped as his eyes fell on her, taking in her homespun dress and prayer cap.

"I knew it!" Ryan yelled, hurrying forward to join her and Beth laughed, blushing. "I knew you'd come back to your old ways. I can't believe I didn't manage to corrupt you!"

He paused and shook his head.

"I did not expect the baby, however," he continued, his eyes falling on her swollen belly. "How much longer until you pop."

Beth giggled.

"Another month or so. What are you doing here, Ryan?" she asked.

"You're not happy to see me?" he teased and Beth shook her head vehemently.

"No! I'm glad to see you. I've been wondering how the restaurant is doing. I keep meaning to take Amos but first my father passed and then I got baptized. Then our wedding..."

"And now a baby," Ryan sighed. "Oh how fast they grow up."

She gave him a warm smile.

"Seriously, what are you doing here? I can't imagine any reason you'd be up here."

"I'm up here because of you," he replied, stepping back to look around. "You and what you've done to this place."

Beth blinked uncomprehendingly.

"What do you mean?"

Ryan's grin widened and he clucked slightly.

"I guess you haven't heard but I have a column in the Food Network Magazine. I've been tasked with finding the best but most obscure locations in America."

Beth blinked.

"Your name has come up in my emails more times than I can count so here I am, ready to do a write up on your place."

"What?"

Ryan nodded.

"Looks like all my training paid off," he teased, winking at her. Excitement flowed through her body and she felt the baby kick slightly with approval.

"Wow," she breathed, a smile touching her face. "I-I don't know what to say."

"Don't say anything," Ryan told her, settling at the counter onto a swivel chair. "Just feed me."

He waved her away dismissively and Beth hurried back into the kitchen to instruct the chefs on what to make.

"What was that all about?" Rachel asked.

"That man used to be my boss in New York. He's here to write a piece on our café for the Food Network Magazine."

Just as Beth's had, Rachel's eyes widened into happy disbelief.

"A write up in the Food Network Magazine?" she breathed. "Soon you'll have your own cooking show!"

Beth chuckled.

"I doubt that," she replied but her heart swelled with happiness. It had been a decade since she'd first left the district in search of something she'd always had right in front of her.

It was a wild ride but I finally found everything I ever wanted and so much more.

HANNAH'S DILEMMA

24

ELIZA BAKER

Part One:

"Two more are gone."

Hannah King kept her eyes trained on the dough she was kneading on the butcher block counter in front of her. Her daed spoke in a low voice to her maemm as the two stood by the back door, and Hannah knew that they didn't want her to hear what they were saying. But she couldn't help but eavesdrop. She knew that they were talking about two more cows being gone. That made it the fourth theft in less than a month.

At first it had only been one cow here or there. No one had noticed at first, but when her daed's prize bull went missing, the family realized that something was wrong. Other families in the neighborhood had also been struck. The men were still trying to figure out how to catch the thief or thieves, but whoever was responsible seemed to be two steps ahead.

"No," Hannah's maemm gasped. "How can this be, Richard?"

Glancing over her shoulder, Hannah saw her daed shrug. The weariness on his face made Hannah's heart break. Who could be doing this to them? She had to believe that it was an Englischer who had a grudge against her family or the community in general. It certainly couldn't be one of their own people. That was absurd.

Hannah looked back to her bread dough before either of her parents caught her watching them. She didn't want to make them feel worse than they already did. Without their prize bull, they needed to raise the money to buy a new one. And Hannah had no idea how that would happen. Normally they would ask the bishop of their church district to dip into the community fund to help them out, but so many people had been hit by the thieves that there wouldn't be enough money to help everyone. Besides, Hannah was fairly certain that her parents didn't want to take money that others needed more.

When her maemm gave a shuddering sigh, Hannah decided that once the bread was rising, she was going to take a prayer walk. She had taken to praying while she took her daily walk, and now she craved the time alone with the Lord. Today she needed the time more than ever because she had a specific prayer request to make: she needed to find a way to help her family.

A moment later her maemm joined her back at the butcher block counter. Hannah glanced up at her quickly, and she could see that her mother had been crying. She was still trying to hold back the tears. Hannah knew that her maemm wasn't going to share with her, so she bit back her questions.

With a final roll of the dough, Hannah was satisfied that she had kneaded the bread thoroughly enough. "Maemm?" she asked. "Would you mind if I went for a walk? I'll be back in plenty of time to finish the bread for supper."

"What? Oh, *da,* of course you can go. Enjoy the nice weather." Her maemm didn't even look up from the vegetables she was chopping as she waved Hannah out of the house.

Hannah washed her hands at the pump sink, straightened her kapp, and hurried out the back door. She saw her daed and her brothers in a circle over by the barn, and she knew that he was telling them about the most recent theft. Her heart cramped in her chest, and she turned away to hurry toward her path in the woods that bordered her family's farm.

Lord, Hannah prayed, *I don't know why this is our cross to bear at the moment, but it is. I can accept that I can't have all the answers right now, but we need your help, Lord. How can I help my family earn more money so that we can replace the livestock that we have lost? How do I convince my parents to let me help? I'm listening, Lord. Amen.*

Wind rustled the leaves of the trees, so Hannah paused. She had learned that the signs of the Lord's presence were all around her if only she would listen. No answers came to her immediately, but she felt peace wash over her so she kept walking.

The trail wound through thick stands of trees as it followed the creek that meandered through the valley that separated her family's farm from that of her beau, Abram. Just thinking about him now sent a flush creeping up her neck. The two had been sweethearts since they were children, and she assumed that eventually the two would marry. Lately, though, he had seemed...distant...almost secretive.

No, she was just being silly, she told herself. She brushed off her concerns, and tried to concentrate on listening to an answer to her questions. Once she'd started thinking about Abram, though, she found that she was too distracted to focus.

A branch snapped to her right, and Hannah froze. There weren't any wild animals that she needed to be worried about. Still, she turned toward the sound, watching, and waiting warily. Another branch snapped, and Hannah felt uneasy for a moment.

"Abram!" she exclaimed as her beau stepped out from behind the trees. Her breath caught in her chest, but she was glad to see him.

"Hannah," Abram said, a frown creasing his forehead as he saw her. She returned his frown. Why didn't he seem happy to see her? "What are you doing out here?"

"Just taking a walk," she said, still frowning at him. "I have a lot to think about, to pray about."

"You should be careful," he said, nodding once before he reached toward her. He pulled her into a quick hug before setting her on her path toward home. "I'll come by later."

And with that he disappeared back into the trees.

Part Two:

The next morning Hannah woke up with a headache. Her maemm and daed had sat all of them down the night before to tell them about the most recent cattle thefts. Hannah had to pretend that she didn't know what they were talking about, but every now and then she had glanced at her brothers and sisters, who all seemed genuinely shocked. She couldn't blame them. After the last set of thefts, the local sheriff had seemed to think that he had caught the person who was responsible. This latest theft proved that theory wrong.

"I don't understand," Mary said. Hannah turned toward her sister who was only eleven months younger than her. The two of them often thought alike, but Mary often said what was on her mind, where Hannah kept her mouth shut, content to watch and listen. Now she was curious to hear what her sister had to say. Mary continued, "The sheriff said that he caught the man responsible, so does this mean that someone else is now stealing our cattle or that they didn't get the right person?"

Their daed shook his head slowly, and Hannah couldn't help but notice how weary he looked as he told them all that he simply didn't have any good answers for them.

Now as Hannah slowly sat up in bed, she realized that Abram had never come by last night. She wondered what had kept him, but she couldn't use up her brain space wondering about that. She still hadn't gotten the answer to her prayers that she had been seeking, and now in the bright morning light, she wondered if that was because she had gotten distracted during her prayer time yesterday. Was the lack of an answer a punishment for not being faithful enough? Hannah knew that she needed to get her chores done so she could get outside to go for another prayer walk.

Hurrying to dress, Hannah noticed that Mary had already awoken. Hannah wondered if her sister had the same sense of urgency to figure out how to help their parents out of this situation. "I'll feed the chickens, Maemm," Hannah called as she whirled through the kitchen.

"No need," her maemm said, halting Hannah's progress as she reached out her hand to the back door. "Mary's already done that. If you could start the eggs for breakfast that would be wonderful."

Hannah didn't hesitate to pull out the large, chipped ceramic bowl that they used to stir the eggs in when they made scrambled eggs for breakfast. After she had cracked twelve eggs, Hannah added some heavy cream that had been brought in from their milk cow, Daisy. That was Hannah's not-so-secret secret for making perfect eggs. She added some salt and pepper before taking the whisk, and beating air into them until the yolks looked light and fluffy.

"Do you mind if I go for a walk after my chores are done?" Hannah asked.

"As long as you are back by dinner time," her maemm answered.

Hannah took the cast iron skillet to the stove, and made the eggs while the rest of her siblings drifted into the kitchen, some fresh in from their morning chores. While they sat down to eat, Hannah's mind drifted to Abram's absence once again. She couldn't help but wonder if something had happened to their cattle. The thought made Hannah's stomach tighten with worry. She would have to stop over there after her prayer walk. Her leg jiggled as she felt her impatience rise. When had her family become such slow eaters?

"Daughter, what is wrong with you this morning? You look like a cat dropped in a bucket of water," her daed said.

Blinking at him in surprise, Hannah shook her head as she flushed. "No, I'm fine. I apologize," she said. "I didn't sleep well. I'm just looking forward to getting outside to tend the garden."

Her daed studied her for a long moment before he nodded. "I heard that Abram has been looking to start his own herd of cattle," he remarked.

Hannah's flush deepened at the implication of that statement. She looked at her plate of eggs and sausage. "I don't know about any of that," she told her family before anyone else could say anything.

"I heard that Abram's daed lost four sheep yesterday," Benjamin announced between forkfuls of egg.

At that news, Hannah's head snapped up. That must have been the reason that Abram hadn't come over last night. She should go over to console the family. Up until now, Abram's family had avoided falling victim to the thefts. Their sheep herd was prized in the community, and Abram's daed had spent his whole life building the herd to be what it was.

It took everything in her to keep her leg still as she finished her breakfast. After everyone had finished eating, Mary offered to help her wash up. When the two of them were alone, Mary asked, "Do you think that Abram is going to propose soon?"

"How should I know?" Hannah asked, feeling the flush rise up her cheeks again. "We haven't really talked about that."

Mary arched an eyebrow. "You've been together for years."

"Oh, fine, we've talked about getting married, and I assume it will happen, but it will have to happen when he's ready," Hannah said. "And if his family has been affected by the thefts, then I don't know when that will be."

Part Three:

Taking a deep breath, Hannah walked up the driveway that led to Abram's house. Her stomach was in knots, and she didn't know how she was going to ask him to help, especially if his own family was now hurting from the rash of thefts. The answer to her prayers had come to her as she had hurried over to Abram's house after she had finished her chores

As she walked she had prayed a quick prayer that she knew wasn't her best one. *Dear Lord,* she prayed, *I know that I'm not praying as deeply as I should, but I need your help. How do I help my family out of this mess? Amen.*

Before she had even had the chance to knock on the front door, it swung open, and Abram's younger sister, Lucy, launched herself at Hannah in a full throttle hug. "Hannah! I haven't seen you in ages," the younger girl cried with delight.

Hannah hugged her back, and couldn't help but chuckle. "Is Abram home?" she asked as Lucy dragged her inside.

"Oh, he's out back helping daed count the sheep. Daed actually thought that four of the sheep had been stolen like all those cattle! Can you believe that?" Lucy exclaimed.

"They weren't?" Hannah asked, confusion slipping through her resolve to ask Abram for help.

"No, they were just lost in the south pasture," Lucy said as she shook her head. "They really caused quite a stir, though. Daed said that your folks lost some more cattle. I'm really sorry about that, Hannah. Do you think they'll ever catch the guy?"

Hannah felt the weight of her family's situation crash down on her, but she did her best to pull a brave smile up on her face. "I sure hope so," she said.

"Sit here and I'll go get the cookies I made this morning," Lucy said, and before Hannah could say anything else, Lucy had disappeared into the kitchen.

Hannah wanted to call after her that really she just wanted to see Abram. The stress of her family's situation was weighing on her so heavily that she needed to share it with someone. She felt God's call before she could put words to it, and in an instant she knew that she needed to share it with the Lord first and foremost.

So while Lucy was still puttering around in the kitchen Hannah bowed her head, and began to pray. *Dear Lord, I'm sorry for my lack of humility. Forgive me for my stupidity. My heart is aching for my parents and for my family. I need your help to bear this cross. I know that you will keep us safe, and guide us through this storm. Amen.*

She finished her prayer just as Lucy came in with a plateful of cookies. A feeling of peace descended on her, and even though she didn't have any more answers than she had started with, she was able to eat a few of the sugar cookies without feeling the need to rush through the visit. Lucy did most of the talking, and Hannah listened with a smile tugging the corners of her mouth.

When they had finished, Hannah stood, and dusted her crumb covered hands on her apron. "I'm just going to pop out back to say hello to Abram. You should stop by our house soon," Hannah told Lucy. "Mary's been making some chocolate chip cookies that you would love"

Slipping through the always warm kitchen, Hannah said hello to Abram's maemm before she stepped out onto the back porch. From where she stood she could see the whole of the farm with the big milking barn and the horse barn, and the small sheds that housed the chickens and goats. Beyond all of that was the large barn that housed the sheep. Green fields spread out in every direction butting up against the woods that separated Abram's family farm from her own family's farm.

She was still looking at the beauty of the farm when she caught sight of Abram and his daed coming out of the barn. They looked like they were deep in conversation so she waited until there seemed to be a lull in their conversation before she waved and called, "Abram!"

Abram turned, and she thought that she saw a frown flit across his handsome features before he waved her toward them. Hannah tried to shake off her moment of unease, before she hurried over. Abram's daed greeted her before he headed back into the house.

"I missed you yesterday," Hannah said.

"Yeah, I'm sorry about that," Abram said. "My daed thought that some of his sheep had been stolen so I had to go out searching for them in the dark. We found them eventually, but it was still a long night."

Something flashed through the edge of Hannah's mind, but she couldn't pin it down. "My daed lost more cattle last night," Hannah said with a sigh.

"I heard about that this morning," Abram said, glancing back at the barn, seeming distracted. "I'm sorry about that."

A bawling cry from the back of the barn drew their attention, and Hannah stepped toward it. Through the dimly lit interior of the barn she could see several calves on the other side. Before she could ask Abram about it, he was already guiding her away.

Still distracted, Hannah blurted, "Abram, you have to help us. How will my family survive all these thefts? We can't afford a new bull."

An uncomfortable look crossed Abram's face, and that discomfort made the thought flit through Hannah's mind again. Something about the way Abram had been so distant lately, and now the way he was shuffling her away from the barn and toward the path home.

"Listen," he said. "I have some things that my daed needs me to attend to, but I promise that I'll stop by later."

And once again, he strode off without another backward glance.

Part Four:

She couldn't believe that she was actually beginning to think that Abram could have anything to do the thefts. Still, as she hurried down the path through the woods, tears blurring her vision, all she could think about were the five new calves in the back stall of the barn. Where had he gotten them? A purchase like that would be big news throughout their community.

Tears burned the backs of her eyes. She had spent so many years assuming that she and Abram would be married and start a family together that she had missed the part where they were growing apart. But had they? Were they? The questions pounded at her temples as she moved faster through the woods.

By the time she got home, she was more confused than ever. Not wanting to let her family see her crying, Hannah made her way to the horse barn where she climbed up into the hay loft. No one would think to look for her there.

The sweet smelling hay surrounded her like a cloud, hiding her away from the rest of the world. The problems that had been swirling around her seemed to drift away for a few moments. When she was a little girl she had come up here after fights with friends or sisters, and when she could spend a few minutes alone with God, she felt better.

God, where are you? She prayed quietly. She didn't want to be a person who lost her faith just because of hardship or strife, but suddenly she felt overwhelmed by the enormity of the situation that she and her family were facing.

Rustling at the foot of the ladder caused Hannah to prop herself up on her elbows. Mary's concerned face popped up over the side of the hayloft floor. Hannah allowed herself to flop back down on to the hay.

"Are you okay?" Mary asked. "I saw you make a beeline over here when you came out of the woods. I thought you might need some company."

Mary climbed into the hay with her, and settled down. The two lay in silence for a long while, and Hannah appreciated her sister's ability to understand her moods. Finally Hannah said, "Do you think that anything will be okay?"

"I'm not sure what exactly you are talking about, but if it's about the cattle thefts, I think it's going to be really hard for maemm and daed to recover. Daed might have to try to find outside work again." Mary paused. "That's not all that you are talking about is it?"

Hannah sighed. "No, it's not. Can I tell you something?"

"Of course," Mary said, propping herself up on her elbow.

"But you can't tell anyone," Hannah said. She took a deep breath. "I think that maybe Abram is involved in the thefts somehow."

"Don't be ridiculous," Mary said. "This is Abram we're talking about."

"He's been so distant lately," Hannah said, barreling on. "And there are at least four new calves in his barn."

Mary got quiet at that news, but she shook her head. "I still think that you aren't seeing the situation clearly. I don't mean to be rude about it, but how can you even think that about Abram. Don't you love him?"

"Of course I do!" Hannah exclaimed, feeling her heart squeeze in her chest.

"Then, I don't understand, how can you suspect him of something so awful?" Mary asked.

Hannah blinked up at the barn's high ceiling. Her sister had a good point. How could she? "I can't explain it," she said. "Even though I love him with all my heart, I guess I've just been looking for an answer so hard that I was willing to see signs everywhere I looked. I was imposing my own will instead of letting God's will be done. I'll have to make a confession before the bishop."

The sisters fell silent again for a long time. "So what are you going to do?" Mary finally asked.

"I don't know," Hannah said. Sitting up, she brushed hay off her dress. "But I'm going to pray about it. And this time, I'm really going to listen with my whole heart."

Part Five:

The darkness pressed in on her, and Hannah pulled her shawl tighter around herself. Hannah knew that she was on a fool's errand, and that she was probably putting herself in harm's way, but she couldn't see any other way. At worst Abram might be involved in the thefts, and at best he had simply been unwilling to help.

She held the flashlight that she had pulled out of her daed's tool chest in the barn, but she was determined not to turn it on until it was absolutely necessary. The moon lent a faint glow to the path around the far pasture, but Hannah was determined to stay near the fence. If she followed the weathered wooden rails, then she knew she wouldn't get lost.

Somewhere in the distance a cow called out, sounding startled. Hannah paused, listening hard for other noises. Hearing nothing, she continued her trek around the pasture fence. When she had thought this plan through she had figured that the best place to watch and wait for the cattle thieves was down by the gate that was closest to the main road. She just hadn't figured out how hard it would be to get over there.

"What do you think you're doing?"

Hannah stifled a scream as she spun around to see Mary carrying a lantern coming up behind her. "Mary! What are you doing here?" Hannah asked in a hushed, exasperated whisper.

"That's exactly what I am asking you," Mary retorted, propping her hand on her hip. The lantern in her other hand bobbed and swung precariously.

"Blow that out," Hannah said, lunging toward her sister. "What if they see it?"

"Who?" Mary asked as she moved the lantern out of her sister's way.

"The cattle thieves," Hannah said. "That's why I'm out here. I want to prove once and for all that Abram isn't involved in this mess, and at the same time find out who is responsible so that we can get our cattle back."

Even in the dim moonlight Hannah could see Mary looking at her in disbelief. "I don't think that's such a good idea," she finally said.

Hannah laughed, and then clapped a hand over her mouth. She looked around quickly. Seeing no one, she turned her attention back to her younger sister. "It's too late for that now," she said. "I need to see this through. I just...I have to know. I hope you can understand that."

"I don't understand," Mary admitted, "but that doesn't affect the fact that I will support you no matter what. I'll come with you. There's strength in numbers after all."

Hannah felt a surge of warmth and love toward her sister. "Thank you," she whispered. "Now the plan is to go around the perimeter of the fence until we get to the gate that leads to the main road. I figure that's the most likely place to see if the cattle thieves come tonight."

As they walked forward Mary asked, "And then what?"

"Honestly, I don't know," Hannah admitted.

"Why do you think they'll come here tonight?" Mary asked.

"I don't know that they'll come here tonight, but I am planning to it here every night until they do come back," Hannah said with more confidence than she felt.

Mary propped her hand on her hip, and sighed. "And then what?" she repeated. "Hannah, if you are going to come up with a harebrained plan, then you have to think it all the way through."

"Actually I'm not sure that I do need to think it all the way through," Hannah said, pressing her lips together to suppress a smile, despite the fact that her sister wouldn't be able to see it anyway. "The definition of harebrained allows me to only think through the first part."

"Hannah, really," Mary said with such exasperation that Hannah couldn't help but giggle. Even in the strange circumstances she found herself in, her sister still made her laugh. "Actions have consequences."

"I know that actions have consequences," Hannah snapped. "But this was all I could think of. Do you have a better suggestion?"

Mary spread out her hands. "I think it's a little late for that, don't you?"

"Well, then you have two choices, you can either stay with me and see what happens, or you can go back home," Hannah said, wrapping her hand around the flashlight before she turned away. I don't have any more choices. I have to find out who is trying to ruin our family, and I need to clear Abram's name."

"Well, obviously I have to come with you," Mary said. "I couldn't live with myself if I went home and then something happened to you."

Hannah nodded, but didn't say anything as she began walking again. Despite the fact that she had been all bluster when suggesting that her sister return to the house, Hannah was secretly glad that her sister was coming with her. There was always safety in numbers...though Hannah wasn't sure that either of them would be safe if they ended up coming face to face with the cattle thieves.

When the two got to the end of the fence, Hannah instinctively dropped down into a crouch. She yanked down her sister, and motioned for Mary to be quiet. Hannah wasn't sure what had caused her to feel like the two of them were threatened, but she knew, she just knew, that there was something out there that made her alert.

A flash of light from the opposite side of the road, near the woods, made Mary gasp beside her, and Hannah gripped her sister's arm. In her mind she was telling herself that they needed to remain quiet, but her body ignored her brain.

Clutching the flashlight in her hand, Hannah let go of her sister, and leapt to her feet. With her heart pounding in her throat, she shouted,

"You! Over there! Stop where you are! I know what you are doing, and I'm not going to let you get away with it!"

Part Six:

"Hannah?"

The sound of total disbelief in Abram's voice made her stomach cramp. She should have known that her discovery was too good to be true. For one triumphant moment, Hannah had been sure that she had caught the cattle thieves. Even as her mind had scrambled to figure out what to do next, she had been thrilled to think that she had finally solved her family's problem. Her heart was beating so hard in her chest that she thought it might break right in front of Abram.

"Yes, it's me," Hannah replied, trying—and failing—to keep the tears out of her voice.

"What are you doing out here?" Abram asked, still sounding confused.

"I could ask the same of you," Hannah said, pushing her broken heart aside. She was going to put an end to this once and for all.

Abram took a step toward her, and Hannah instinctively took a step back. She hated that this was how she was acting with the man she loved—-and she did still love him dearly—but all the evidence that she had at her disposal pointed to Abram being the culprit.

"It isn't safe for you to be out here," Abram said, stepping closer.

"Why?" Hannah asked. She needed him to tell her the truth, even if it wasn't something that she wanted to hear.

"If the cattle thieves show up again—" Abram was cut off by the sound of an engine revving in the distance. Swiftly, he grabbed the flashlight out of her hand, clicked it off, and pulled her down below the fence line so that they wouldn't be seen.

Hannah's heart began to pound in her chest, and her temples began to throb as she realized that even though she didn't know exactly what was going on, she had her evidence that Abram wasn't involved. But, then, why was he out here so late at night?

When she asked him that exact question, she could feel him grimace. "I should be asking you the same thing," he muttered. "But I'm out here as part of a community patrol that your daed set up. We've been watching for the cattle thieves at different farms for weeks, but so far we haven't been able to catch them."

Hannah's cheeks flamed with embarrassment and shame. "Abram, I have something to tell you," she said softly.

"What? Are you going to confess that you're one of the cattle thieves?" he asked.

The humor in his voice only made the situation worse. Taking a deep breath, Hannah said, "I thought you might be involved. In the thefts, I mean. I don't know why. Well, maybe I do. I was so worried about my family that I was looking for an answer wherever I could see one. I'm so sorry. When you started to get distant, I didn't know what to think. And I thought the worst. I understand if you are angry with me. And I understand if you never want to see me again."

To her amazement, Abram burst out in laughter that he quickly stifled. "I don't mean to laugh at you," he said with all the seriousness he could muster. "But why didn't you just come to me with your concerns? We could have cleared all this up, and you wouldn't have had to feel the need to come out in the middle of the night to stalk dangerous cattle thieves."

"You're still teasing me," Hannah pointed out, although she was beginning to feel herself relax.

"Maybe just a little," Abram admitted. "But only because you seem so upset."

"Well, I thought that you might be destroying my family's livelihood, so I think that it will take a moment longer before I feel cheerful again," Hannah said. She heard the distress still in her voice, creeping out as she spoke.

"It does hurt that you would think that of me," Abram said after a long moment of silence. "But I can understand that you needed to put the pieces together."

Hannah stepped forward, and reached out to take Abram's hand. "I am sorry that I suspected you," she said. "But I'm sorrier that I didn't come talk to you about my concerns. Well...I did try one day, but you and your daed were busy, and then I saw the calves, and well..."

"You saw the calves?" Abram's voice sounded choked and higher than normal. "You weren't supposed to see the calves."

Another shot of fear went through Hannah's stomach. Could it be that Abram was still somehow involved in the cattle thievery? Could he be lying to her? She thought through the conversation that they had just had, and she decided that she knew Abram. She knew his heart, and she had been praying for answers. She loved him, and she knew that she had been wrong to doubt him. She still had a lot of questions, though, and she knew that she needed to be bold to ask him.

"I saw the calves," she confirmed. "What were they for Abram? How did you find the money to buy four calves? I thought...I thought that you were saving for our future."

Abram sighed, and dropped Hannah's hand so he could run both hands through his hair. In the dim light of the glow from the flashlight, she could see the hair sticking up in all different directions. She thought that he looked as frazzled as she felt.

"They were, are, for our future," Abram said. "The calves, I mean. They are for our future. I took out a loan from my daed to buy them. I'm going to raise them, sell them, and after I pay back my daed, buy some more. I just thought that it would be better to make a small profit before I told you about them, but I can see now that I should have shared my thoughts with you."

"That would have been nice," Hannah agreed. "But I guess I can see why you did that."

A silence descended upon them, but Hannah still had other questions. She still had other thoughts that she needed to share with him, but she knew that now wasn't the time for a long conversation. Suddenly she was aware of the other men from the community patrol milling about on the edge of her vision, along with her daed and Mary. If she hadn't been so intent on getting answers, she would have felt intense embarrassment.

"When were you going to tell me?" Hannah asked, deciding that was the next right question that she wanted an answer to.

Abram shuffled his feet, and said," Right after I proposed to you."

Hannah knew that she had heard him correctly, but she had to ask him anyway. "When were you going to propose to me?"

"I was planning on doing it soon, but I thought it might be better as a surprise," Abram said. "But I suppose this is as good a spot as anywhere."

As his words sank into her brain, Hannah felt her heart beat faster, the sound of blood throbbing in her ears drowning out all the noise around them. He was going to ask her to marry him right now, in this moment. And then she realized that he was actually doing it. She heard him say, "I'd be honored if you'd be my wife."

"Yes," Hannah said as it echoed through her heart. "But wait. Can we really do this here? Now?"

Abram laughed. "Of course we can."

"But we're all out here trying to catch cattle thieves," Hannah groaned. "What if they came around the corner right now? They could be heavily armed. They could hurt all of us."

"We're fine," Abram said. "The thieves seem to have a pattern. None of us think that they'll try anything tonight, and if they did we are more than ready for them. This, right here, the two of us are more important than any of that."

"Then yes," Hannah said feeling her worries break away and elation rise up in her chest like she hadn't in weeks. "I would absolutely love to be your wife."

After the two of them had hugged, Hannah hurried over to her sister and her daed to tell them what had just transpired. While her daed went to talk to Abram and to shake his hand. When their daed had gone, Mary grabbed Hannah with a small squeal, and said, "So I guess he wasn't stealing our cattle, huh?"

Embarrassment raced through Hannah, but she knew that the Lord had given her all the answers she needed, and that she needed to be humble in her mistakes. "Of course not," she said. "I was wrong, but that's all part of being human. God has led us to this point, and He will continue to lead us wherever we need to go."

As she glanced over at Abram and her daed, Hannah was struck by the exact answer to her prayers, her past and her future blending seamlessly together. And she realized that by trusting the Lord, even with the uncertainties of life, she didn't have any reason to fear.

BETHANY

Bethany felt a sharp nudge at her ribs and she quickly blinked the sleep from her eyes, startled.

"Beth, look at that!" Andrea whispered, leaning across her half-awake frame to point out the tiny window. Bethany turned her head to look out the pane and her breath caught in her throat. The plane was descending over the most breathtaking landscape which she had ever seen.

That isn't saying much, Bethany thought with dry amusement. *This is the first time I have ever been out of Indiana in my life. Still, I can't imagine that it gets much more lovely than this.*

She watched as steaming mountaintops passed beneath them and they flew above lush, green jungles as far as the eye could see.

"Attention ladies and gentlemen," a flight attendant said over the intercom. "We will be landing in Managua in fifteen minutes. Please ensure that your trays are in the upright position and your seatbelts are fastened."

Bethany checked her waist quickly for the strap and sat back against the seat. The flight had been less scary than she had anticipated. She had rather enjoyed the journey through the clouds.

It's a little bit like being next to God, Bethany thought. She cast a sidelong look at Andrea who was still straining over her lap to take in the scenery.

She is so excited about this trip. I wonder why she does these missions so often. You would think she would be discouraged by the futility behind them. No matter how many supplies we send or hours we volunteer, the locals continued to be sick but the thousands. It's like ramming your head against a wall.

For Bethany's part, she had been basically blackmailed into joining the church group on that excursion. Pastor Frank had pulled her aside one afternoon after choir practice.

"Your voice has become more lovely with each passing year, Bethany," he told her appreciatively. "We are so blessed to have you in our choir."

"Thank you, Pastor," she replied, smiling demurely. She was pleased by the young Reverend's compliment. Like the other young ladies in the parish, she had somewhat of a school girl's crush on James Frank. He was still unmarried and there was a playful competition among the women to see who might be able to win his affections. Yet as the years melted by, it became apparent that Pastor Frank had no mind for marriage, at least not to any of the single women in his midst. Still, Bethany could not help but feel flattered by his kind words.

"Bethany, I wanted to ask you about something," Pastor Frank continued and Bethany turned her green eyes to stare up at him.

"Sure," she replied. "Ask away."

Pastor Frank cleared his throat and looked uncomfortably at his shoes. Bethany was immediately filled with a sense of caution.

Uh oh…is he speaking on behalf of my parents?

"We have a mission upcoming to Nicaragua," he said slowly, maintaining his gaze on the floor. Bethany was already shaking her dark hair. Every time a trip was planned to some God forsaken third world environment, he tried to recruit her. Bethany could think of nothing less appealing than spending two weeks in a suffocating country, encased in flies. It was not that Bethany was heartless. She volunteered at the church's soup kitchen every second weekend and worked as a camp counsellor with the developmentally challenged in the summer. Bethany was thrilled to help in any way she could; at home.

"Before you refuse, Bethany, I should tell you that we will be forced to cancel the trip if we don't find one more body. You have never gone on a mission, have you?"

"No, I haven't," Bethany agreed. "And I have no interest in going now."

Pastor Frank shook his head sadly.

"I know how you feel about these excursions, Bethany but I wouldn't be asking if you weren't my only hope."

Bethany gritted her teeth and stared at her hands. She knew that Jeanie Williams would typically be the sixth person to go but she had just had a baby. She wracked her brain for anyone else to replace Jeanie but she was coming up blank. She imagined that Pastor Frank had already done the same.

"I wouldn't be asking you if we had another option, Beth," Pastor Frank assured her. "I promise you, this will be a life changing experience for you. When you see the children's faces light up, it will all be worth it."

If I say no, they will cancel the trip and everyone will be angry at me, Bethany thought miserably. *There really isn't much of a choice, is there?*

Bethany sighed heavily.

"When do we leave?"

As the aircraft descended into the surreal beauty of Managua, Bethany could not help but feel a spark of excitement.

"I hope Dr. Martinez is still here," Andrea breathed as the landing gear touched the runway. "In all the missions I have ever done, he is the best doctor I have ever seen. The children love him and he is so caring."

Bethany rolled her eyes.

"He's a doctor, Andy. That's basically in his job description," she replied.

Andrea's eyes clouded over as she shook her head.

"You would think so," Andrea answered sadly. "But the stress of the job gets to most of them. The death and sickness turns what were probably great doctors into robots. I have been to countries where they treat their patients like an assembly line. One physician in Liberia actually would scream, 'next!' and shove the patient off the bed to make room for another. It was horrifying." Bethany was shocked but she was certain Andrea was exaggerating. Doctors were well paid for their roles. Why else would someone become a doctor?

"Ladies and gentleman, we have arrived in Managua, Nicaragua. The temperature here is a balmy 101 degrees and the sun is shining. We hope you had a pleasant flight aboard American Airlines flight 867 and we thank you for flying with us. Have a lovely stay in Nicaragua."

One hundred and one degrees? What kind of hell on earth have we flown into? Bethany thought woefully. Her mood was already souring at the thought of the heat.

Slowly, seatbelts came off and Andrea rose into the aisle to allow for Bethany to follow her onto the runway tarmac. The women blinked at the intense rays of sun as they descended the stairs. Bethany's legs were cramped from the four-hour flight and she realized she was thirsty.

"Do you have any water," she asked Andrea as they walked into the Augusto C. Sandino International Airport. Andrea nodded and dug a bottle from inside her carryon bag. Bethany took a swig and wiped her brow. She was already sweating.

They walked toward the luggage carousel to wait for their bags. The rest of their group had arrived the previous day with the supplies. Andrea and Bethany had been unable to get on that flight which was fine with Bethany. It just meant one less day that she would be stuck in Central America.

"Oh, there's one of yours, Beth," Andrea told her, gesturing at the bags. Instantly, a young boy appeared at her side. Bethany guessed him to be no older than eight. He was filthy and wore a flimsy, holey t-shirt. His knees were scarred and thin in a pair of shorts that were swimming trunks and much too large for his small form. His flip flops were as good as bare feet, they had eroded so badly. He offered Bethany and Andrea a bright smile.

"I help!" he declared, rushing to grab the bag.

"No, wait!" Bethany yelled but Andrea put her hand on her companion's arm and shook her head.

"Just let him get it," she whispered. "He's only looking to make a dollar."

Bethany was alarmed as she watched the frail boy struggle with the luggage. She rushed over to assist him with wrestling the bag over the belt. Panting, the child waved her away.

"I have," he told her. "More?"

Swallowing, Bethany nodded and pointed out their other belongings. The child refused any more help, almost knocking himself over with the heavy items.

He is too small to be doing this, she thought, but she did not interfere. She glanced at Andrea and she could see the compassion in the older woman's face.

When they had claimed their belongings, the boy piled up the mound and rolled behind them, still beaming happily. Bethany desperately wanted to sent the boy on his way but Andrea seemed content having him assist.

They cleared customs and exited the gate, the boy faithfully at their side.

"How long is he going to carry our bags?" Bethany finally whispered to Andrea, her heart breaking.

"Until they are loaded into a car safely," she replied calmly but Bethany could see she was as affected by the child's struggling as she.

Bethany clamped her mouth closed.

She has more experience in these things than I do but still...

"Andrea!" A tall, intelligent looking man was hurrying toward them, the beam on his tired face lighting the dusty airport. Andrea squealed in a childlike fashion, causing Bethany to give her a strange look. She had never seen her friend look so excited. The man approached and embraced Andrea warmly. He stepped back and Bethany examined him furtively.

Ah, this is probably the doctor she was talking about on the plane, Bethany thought, eyeing the handsome man. He wore thin green scrubs which were worn with age but it brought out the warm glow of his bronze skin and wavy black hair. His eyes were wide and cat-shaped with extremely long lashes, framing a set of intense, brown eyes. He was taller than Bethany expected, towering over both the women but at least six inches.

"Dr. Martinez, this is Bethany Grieger. This is her first mission anywhere so you will have to show her some extra attention," Andrea joked. The doctor rested his eyes on Bethany, his eyes lighting up as he stared at her expressive jade eyes.

"Welcome to Managua, Betany," he said cordially, offering her a long hand. "I hope this will not be your last trip with us."

Bethany accepted it, relishing his lilting accent and his inability to pronounce the "h" in her name.

"Nice to meet you, Dr. Martinez," she told him. Their gazes locked for a moment and time seemed to slow momentarily. He broke the spell, turning his attention the boy with the luggage.

"I see you have met Dario," he said, ruffling the child's hair. Dario smiled up at the doctor.

"Hola, doctor," Dario smiled. The two exchanged a few words in Spanish before Dr. Martinez gestured for the women to follow them

"Excuse me for speaking in our native tongue," he told them apologetically. "Dario's sister has been very sick and I wanted to know how she was doing. Unfortunately, his English is not fluent."

"What is wrong with his sister?" Bethany asked as they made their way back into the sunshine.

"She is suffering from cholera," Dr. Martinez answered sadly and Bethany gasped.

"Oh, how awful! How old is she?"

Dario began to load the bags into a beat-up VW bus, his smile never wavering.

"She is five but luckily she is on the upswing," Dr. Martinez replied. Dario finished heaving the luggage into the back of the van and turned to the group. Andrea already had a bill in her hand which she deposited into Dario's small palm. The boy looked at the crumpled paper in his hand, his mouth dropping open.

"Oh, gracias, senora! Muchas gracias!" he almost sobbed, clutching the money. His dark eyes were filled with grateful tears and he scampered off as if he was worried Andrea was going to change her mind.

"How much did you give him?" Bethany asked as they jumped into the vehicle.

"I only gave him five dollars but that's as good as a hundred-dollar bill around here," she murmured back. Again, Bethany was overcome with sadness.

Dr. Martinez took the wheel and began to drive out of the airport area. Bethany marveled at how laid back the travellers seemed. It was contrary to anything she had ever seen in the United States. No one seemed to be in a rush to go anywhere. As if reading her thoughts, Dr. Martinez spoke.

"Our way of life is quite a bit different than that you are accustomed," he told her. "Nicaragua is the second poorest country in the western hemisphere. Our major exports are coffee, tobacco, sugar and gold but of course those products are very weather and climate dependant. Tourism has increased in the past decade so we are told our economy is on the rise however, there is still much disease and a need for clean water."

Bethany leaned forward between the front seats to absorb every word.

"I thought that there were many fresh water lakes in this country," Bethany piped up and Dr. Martinez nodded.

"That is true but they are mostly infested with bacteria. We simply don't have the resources to filter the water. Most people drink from the lakes and end up with E-coli, parasites and in the case of Dario's sister, Luz, cholera."

Bethany was aghast.

"We have to do something about that!" she cried passionately and both Andrea and the doctor chuckled gently.

"There simply is not the money," he said sadly. "But God sends us angels like you to make things easier sometimes."

They were silent for the remainder of the trip, Bethany lost in thought as the lush but impoverished setting slipped before her wide eyes.

They don't have clean water and they get sick from it. If they don't have money for clean water, they definitely don't have money for the medicine to cure them of the illnesses. It makes more sense for them to spend the money on the water than it does to pay for the aftermath of drinking tainted liquid. But if there is no money, how do we make this happen?

Bethany had no answer.

When they arrived at their hotel, Bethany was immediately repulsed. The three-story building was crumbling from the inside out. Their room was miniscule and stifling hot.

"Where is the bathroom?" she asked Andrea, dropping her case reluctantly onto the floor beside one of the twin beds.

"It's a common bathroom down the hall," she replied, plopping heavily onto the bed. A huge insect scurried out from its hiding spot, causing Bethany to scream. Andrea laughed.

"You better get used to the bugs," she teased. "There are creatures you can't imagine in these parts. And lizards as big as your head."

Bethany shuddered, eyeing the scuttling insect. She closed her eyes and took a deep breath.

I can do this for thirteen more days, she told herself. *Just focus on the sick kids and forget about the twenty-six-legged animal under your bed.*

Bethany was sure she wouldn't sleep for the remainder of the trip.

"Get changed. We have to get to the clinic," Andrea pressed. "We have to meet the others soon."

Bethany nodded and headed into the hallway to find the washroom. The plumbing was ancient and everything leaked from the sink to the toilet. The shower consisted of a drain over a set of floor tiles and a long hose.

I wonder if this water is safe for showering.

She wet a washcloth and wiped her face carefully, avoiding her orifices lest the water was contaminated. She would have to ask Andrea about it.

Or I can ask the doctor, Bethany thought, her mind recalling the wisdom and depth of his brown eyes. *I bet he knows everything.*

Bethany returned to the room and slipped into a simple white sundress.

"What do we do at the clinic?" she asked, waiting for Andrea to get ready.

"We will devise a plan. Half of us will go to the church for the first week and supply the children with books, pencils, papers and other necessities for school. We'll do activities with the kids, just as we do at home in Sunday school. The second week, we will switch and stay at the clinic helping the doctors with the sick. Dr. Martinez will show you what needs to be done there. We'll figure out which group you and I will fall into when we meet the others today."

Bethany was surprised to find herself hoping she was on clinic duty.

I am interested to see how medicine is handled in the third world, she told herself but she knew she was lying. She wanted to spend more time with the attractive doctor. She had only spent moments with Dr. Martinez but she found him intriguing. His work was thankless and never ending yet he maintained an almost cheerful aura as if he was unaffected by the endless suffering in which he was surrounded.

Andrea turned to her and waved a chubby hand.

"I'm ready, Beth. Let's go – the car will be waiting."

When they arrived at the Managua Children's Clinic, Bethany was taken aback. The air of serenity which had floated over Managua, shadowing them from the airport had evaporated. In its place was havoc. In every corner of the tiny building lay children in various stages of agony. Some were vomiting on the floor, others were clinging to their defeated looking mothers. The stench of disease and urine wafted into her nose but Bethany was too wrapped up in the mollifying sights to notice the putrid stench. While a few small beings were lucky enough to have claimed beds, the majority were laying on the floor. Almost all of them were crying. Bethany fought back her own tears, springing into action.

"What can I do?" she cried to Andrea. To her surprise, the older woman stood back, her mouth turned down in grief.

"Just wait. The doctor will tell us what to do," she replied but Bethany could barely hear her above the din.

"We just can't stand here!" Bethany insisted. "We have to do something!"

Andrea shook her head and her shoulders sagged.

"It is always like this," she replied, anguish in her voice. "All we can do is wait for Dr. Martinez to tell us what to do or else we may be more of a hindrance than a help."

As if on cue, the doctor hurried up to them.

"Ah wonderful! You have arrived. How is your hotel?" Bethany stared at him in disbelief.

How can he ask about our hotel when these children are in such pain?

But as she had the thought, she quickly realized he was simply trying to put them at ease.

"Fine," she replied shortly. "What can I do here?"

Nodding approvingly at her eagerness to get started, he handed her a pair of scrubs and another pair to Andrea.

"After you have put these on, go around to all of the children and try to have them drink a few sips of water. Do not give them too much or they will vomit and it will not only be counterproductive, it will be a waste of good water. There are cases of bottled water which your group brought in my office yesterday. I have the key and you will need to come to me for it every time you need more bottles. I have the only copy. It is important that you keep whatever bottles you have on you at all times or they will be stolen."

Bethany stared at him in shock.

"Who will steal bottles of water from sick children?" she choked in disbelief. Dr. Martinez shrugged as if the information was commonplace.

"These are desperate times, Betany. The children you see here are merely the tip of the iceberg. There are many who live too far away to come here for medical attention. Their families are just as desperate to see them well as the families you see here."

Bethany paled, thinking of impoverished children laying untreated in remote areas of the country, waiting for certain death.

"What happens to them? They are just left to die?" Bethany demanded, gulping at the thought. Dr. Martinez shook his head and smiled.

"No, of course not. I will go to the rural areas three times a week after I leave the clinic to tend to those children also. Luz, Dario's sister is one of my out patients. If I get word of a sick child, I attend to them right away but oftentimes, I am not notified until it is much too late."

Bethany was overcome with emotions so strong, she was almost brought to her knees.

When does this man sleep? He works all day and then travels around at night to do the same, horrific work.

He seemed to read her mournful expression and offered her another kind smile.

"Sometimes they get well," he told her, handing her the key. "We must focus on the positive because that is all we have." She nodded and snapped to attention, hurrying toward the office. She threw on the scrubs and armed herself with several bottles of water which she found piled in a corner.

There are not nearly enough bottles here, she thought, looking hopelessly at the cases. She returned to the exterior of the clinic and knelt next to the nearest child.

"Hi, honey," she whispered to the little girl of about two. The child stared up at her with hollow, hurting eyes and Bethany fought the urge to sob.

"Have some water," she offered, pressing the bottle to her parched lips. The baby tried to struggle against her but Bethany held her firmly and managed to get a few drops of water into her.

"Rest now," she whispered, stroking her tiny face. As if she understood, her lids closed heavily. Bethany moved on to the next child and, sweetly feeding him the clean liquid.

Bethany had been at it for over an hour, oblivious to everything but the little bodies in her care when someone tapped her shoulder. Slightly annoyed at the distraction, Bethany peered up and found herself staring into Dr. Martinez's deep eyes. Her irritation dissolving, she rose to her feet.

"I'm sorry to interrupt you, Miss Betany," he told her, his thick Spanish accent still unable to handle the "h" in her name. "But you forgot to return the key to me."

Apologetically, Bethany reached into the small pocket in her scrubs to retrieve the office key.

"I'm sorry," she told him, handing it back to him. "I am just on my way over there now anyway. I need more water."

Dr. Martinez looked around appreciatively.

"You managed to get a lot of them to drink," he remarked. "That is no easy feat. Most are feeling so ill, they will not accept anything orally."

Bethany lowered her head humbly.

"They did not fuss very much," she told him. "I fear they are too sick to argue."

The two turned back to the office and Dr. Martinez unlocked the door to allow them to enter.

"Dr. Martinez – "

He faced her abruptly.

"Please call me Jasiel," he told her. Bethany felt a small fission of pleasure course through her as he said his name. His fixed his penetrating eyes upon her and she felt her cheeks stain pink under his gaze.

"Jasiel," she continued, trying to force the blush from her cheeks. "Where do you get aid from if things are so dire in your country?"

He pursed his lips together as he dug through the drawers looking for something.

"Mostly we depend on emergency relief from other countries. The United States in a big provider in assistance. The biggest problem we face, unfortunately, is that we simply do not have enough medical staff to deal with the sick."

Bethany busied herself collecting more bottles, her mind racing with thoughts.

We will have to do something about this.

The week seemed to fly by, the days blurring together one after the other. There was no time to explore the ancient and mystic city of Managua as the group worked tirelessly from sun up to sun down at the clinic. Even though she was in the company of her fellow church friends, Bethany barely saw them except briefly in the mornings and evenings at meals. When they finally made it back to the hotel, they inhaled supper and generally fell into a deep, exhaustive slumber. Bethany's concern that she would be unable to sleep with the critters with whom she was rooming proved unfruitful. The lizards had begun to grow on her with their nonchalant expressions and beady little eyes.

The only constant that Bethany had was Jasiel who seemed to take special interest in helping her adjust. He allowed her to perform basic medical procedures, despite her protests.

"I have no training!" she had cried the first time he handed her a needle. The handsome doctor had shaken his head wryly, pressing the instrument into her hand.

"Then you are still more qualified than most of the people whom we have here," he replied. Gulping, Bethany had accepted and under his careful guidance, she began administering much needed medicine to the children.

On the fourth day, little Lilliam rose to her feet and walked for the first time. She had been in the clinic for two weeks, unable to move.

"Jasiel!" Bethany screeched. "Lilliam is walking!"

He had nodded stoically but his face registered relief.

"Thank God," he whispered. "I was beginning to lose faith in her chances for survival."

Bethany impulsively embraced him in a hug before attending to the child. She did not see the look of longing gave to her disappearing back.

Later that evening as they began to close the clinic, Jasiel took her aside and out of earshot of Andrea and Jack who were stripping the linens from the beds.

"It was because of you that Lilliam finally was able to move from bed," he told her solemnly. Pleased but unwilling to take the credit, Bethany shook her head.

"No, it was God's hand at work here," she told him.

"Yes, it was God who sent you to us but it was your attention to that child which made her well again. If we had only a few more people to spend the time with these babies..."

Bethany did not know how to respond. She looked into his eyes, wanting desperately to end his suffering as much as he wished to end that of the children. He gave her a weak smile and again, Bethany was affected by a shiver.

Over and above his tireless efforts, he must be very lonely. He spends most of his time alone or surrounded by children. I wonder how his wife feels about him being gone so often.

Bethany decided to ask.

"How does your wife handle your hours?" she blurted out. He raised an eyebrow in surprise.

"I am not married. No woman in her sane mind would stand for the type of work I have committed myself to." He paused and looked at Bethany thoughtfully. "I thought you would have figured out that I was unmarried by now."

A rush of heat colored Bethany's cheeks under his wistful stare. She dropped her head in embarrassment.

He feels it too, she thought, her heart pounding in her chest. *We have a connection but it can never be...can it?*

"Beth! Dr. Martinez is here!" Andrea called from the doorway later that evening. Bethany almost tripped over her feet in her rush to the threshold. Andrea tried to step out of her way but the size of the room made the dance almost impossible. Eventually, Andrea ended up behind the flimsy wooden door. Jasiel stood in the hallway appearing exhausted.

"Jasiel, what are you doing here?" she asked, shooting Andrea a covert glance. The woman raised her eyebrow questioningly.

"Jasiel?" she mouthed silently, trapped in her spot but Bethany ignored her.

"I hope you will forgive the intrusion, Betany," he said. "But I am about to head into the rural areas. I thought you might wish to join me and meet some of the children outside of the city."

Eagerly, Bethany nodded. She had been wondering about the children outside the city. Her plan had been to ask to accompany him later in the week but it seemed that he had read her mind.

"I would love to!" she exclaimed and Jasiel nodded happily. "I'll be back later, Andy."

Andrea shrugged her shoulders and collapsed on the bed.

"I'll likely be sound asleep," she replied, already closing her eyes.

The drive from Managua to Masaya took forty-five minutes in Jasiel's old van and it was the first time Bethany had an opportunity to see the incredible Nicaraguan countryside. Bethany's breath was stolen by the towering palms and the untouched landscape.

"This is what the dinosaurs saw!" Bethany proclaimed, staring open-mouthed at the mountains against the glorious sunset. Jasiel chuckled.

"Yes, we do not have much industry in Nicaragua," he agreed.

As night began to fall, the smooth fields became a sprinkling of dilapidated shanties and Jasiel pulled his car to a stop. A sudden fear seized Bethany as people began to poke their heads from the depth of the seemingly abandoned properties.

"There are people in there," she whispered as Jasiel collected supplies. He glanced at her, realizing she was serious.

"Yes, Betany. This is where people live," he told her.

Just when I thought I could not be any more shocked by the living conditions in this country, Bethany thought, gritting her teeth. She quickly began to assist the doctor and followed him up to a tin shack. Immediately, the door flew open and Dario stood, his eyes red from crying. He began to babble in Spanish and was joined by an older woman. The two barraged Jasiel with words which Bethany could not understand but she recognized the urgency in their tone.

"What happened?" she whispered, almost running after Jasiel into the house. He did not need to answer. Laying on a pallet on the floor was a small girl in the throes of eternal sleep. A hand flew to Bethany's mouth as she gasped back a sob. It was Dario's sister, Luz.

The doctor leaned forward to check for signs of life but there were none. Luz was gone.

Bethany wanted to scream, to cry out and yell at God but she did none of those things. This was not about her deep regret. Dario and his mother had lost a small, precious soul and their anguish was fresh and real. Immediately, Bethany reached out to embrace Dario who clung to her like a burr. She whispered calmingly into his ear as he cried, his frail body trembling in shock.

Jasiel scooped up Luz's lifeless body and walked her to the van while Bethany stroked Dario's hair. When he returned, he spoke to the family in low tones and nodded at Bethany to follow him.

"We must return to Managua to arrange for Luz's body to be cremated," Jasiel told her. "The family has no means to provide for a proper burial."

His voice was raw with grief. Bethany slowly reclaimed her seat on the passenger's side of the car and lowered her gaze so she would not see Luz's mother chasing after the van, calling out for her daughter.

On the sixth day, it was time for the group to switch. Bethany was supposed to join Andrea and Jack at the church but as she reluctantly geared up for the switch that morning at the hotel, there was a knock at the door.

Aimee Thompson, the mission co-ordinator wanted to speak with Bethany.

"There's been a change of plans if it's okay with you," Aimee told her. Bethany stared at her quizzically.

"Dr. Martinez has requested that you stay at the clinic for the remainder of the trip. He says that the children have become very attached to you and honestly, it's not fair to upset them any more than they've already been upset. Is that something you can live with?" Aimee asked. Bethany nodded with too much enthusiasm.

"Oh, yes ma'am!" she declared. "I can definitely stay at the clinic for the rest of the trip!"

As Aimee left, Andrea shot Bethany a sly smile.

"I'm sure it's only for the good of the children," Andrea joked. "It has nothing to do with the handsome, attentive doctor who seems to stare at you everywhere you go."

"Of course it's for the children!" Bethany retorted angrily. "What a horrible suggestion that I am using sick kids for a romantic interest."

Andrea lost the smile and shook her head.

"I would never say that. I know your heart and intentions are true, Beth. I would also have to be deaf, blind and dumb not to see the way you and Dr. Martinez have connected...or can I call him Jasiel also?"

Bethany grimaced. Luz's death had a much bigger impact on her than she had expected, affecting her mood substantially. She had thrown herself completely into the care of the children, staying well after the others had gone back to the hotel for the night. She and Jasiel had become joined at the hip and while Luz had been the one that got away, other boys and girls seemed to be thriving in the short time since she had arrived.

"Well, I hope you don't become too attached, Beth. You're going to be heartbroken when it's time to go home," Andrea commented casually. Bethany felt the blood drain from her face. She had purposely avoided thinking about the impending departure but Andrea's words had forced the unwanted thoughts into mind.

What will I do when it is time to leave?

On the last night the group was to be in Nicaragua, Jasiel appeared at the hotel again. This time Bethany answered the door. Her heart was an explosion of bittersweet emotion as she stared into his soulful eyes.

"Would do you do me the honor of having dinner with me this evening?" he asked her. Not trusting her voice, Bethany nodded and allowed for Jasiel to lead her into the city. He had arranged for a romantic table inside a small, cozy restaurant.

As soon as they were seated, he grasped her hands.

"Betany, I want you to know that these last two weeks have been the best since I began my medical career. I have never been so in tune with anyone or met another person who seemed to care about the children as much as I do."

Bethany forced a lump down her windpipe and willed herself not to cry.

"I know we are worlds apart but I wanted to let you know how I feel before you leave. I hope you will consider coming back on another trip."

Bethany blinked the tears from her eyes.

"What has happened here has exceeded my wildest imagination," she told him seriously, squeezing his palms. "I have never felt more enlightened or awake..."

Or in love, she added silently. They shared a melancholic smile and forced themselves to concentrate on their last moments together, pushing the impending unhappiness of tomorrow from their minds.

"That was a lovely trip," Andrea commented, as the plane began to taxi down the runway. She nodded absently, staring toward the airport.

"I think that we are making some progress here, though, don't you?" Andrea asked. Her question went unanswered and she sighed heavily.

"Hello? Are you ignoring me for any particular reason?"

She turned to face Andrea and smiled sheepishly.

"Sorry. I am just wondering if we made the right decision allowing Bethany to stay behind," Aimee replied. Andrea laughed.

"I don't think we had much of a choice," Andrea replied. "Short of dragging her on the plane, she was staying."

Aimee nodded absently, a sweet smile touching her lips. She raised her eyes toward the ceiling of the aircraft and winked.

"You know what you're doing up there," she told the heavens.